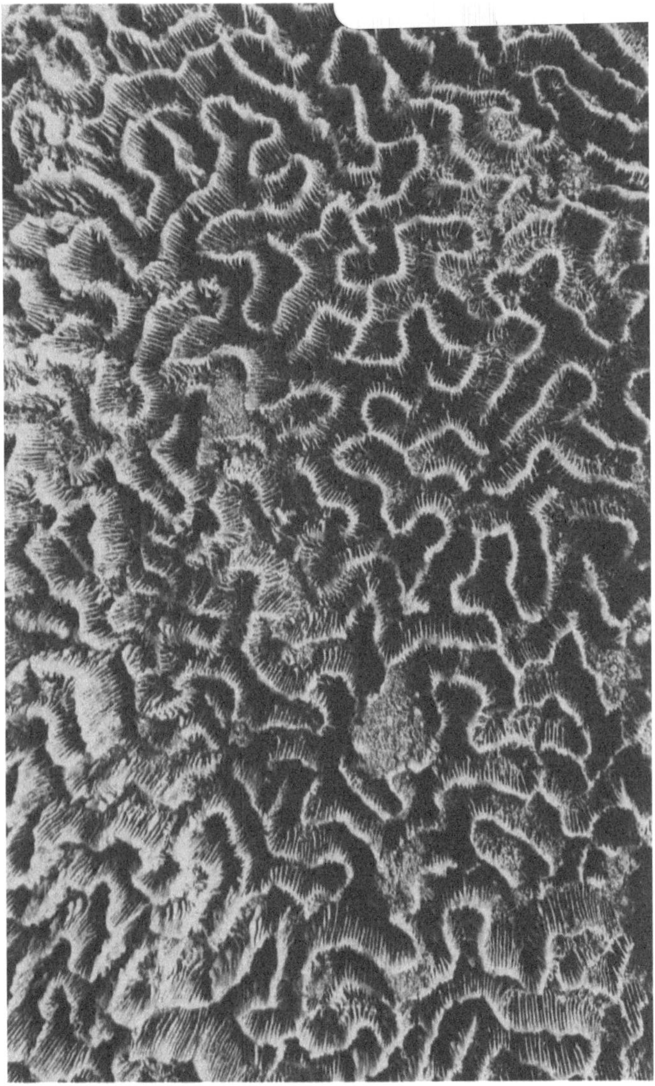

WRITTEN BY SILENCE

∘ Tales From The Divine ∘

Inscribed & Edited by Sean Aeon

Written by Silence: Tales From The Divine. Copyright © 2025 by Sean Aeon. All rights reserved. No part of this book may be used or reproduced in any manner whatsoever without written permission except in the case of brief quotations embodied in critical articles and reviews.

ISBN 978-1-959810-23-0

LCCN 2025918827

Original Photography & Cover Art by:
Sean Aeon

www.aeonaes.com

AEONAES.COM

• ART & INSIGHT •

∘ Table Of Contents ∘

° Written With Reverence °

Angels & Fallen Angels.

* * * * * * * *

Praise.

As I walked The Messenger back to his car, he almost tripped on a small group of wild Dandelions. After easily surviving the unlikely entanglement, he mentioned an old landlord who drowned plants in "weed killer", if they weren't the ones they personally planted.

How mundane habits were executed, was often an expression of underlying perceptions many were unaware of.

Those who were loudest about what wasn't understood, were quiet about their uncertainty, ignorance, and fear.
There was nothing on Earth—produced by Earth—requiring correction, while some were afforded the opportunity to evolve.

Chaos didn't occur naturally, chaos didn't occur at all; there was only harmony.

Harmony was created once, then allowed to be witnessed for eternity.
Each moment in time was comprised of the moments leading up to it.
Every experience and interaction was able to be traced to its point of origin, with the use of meditative-listening (probing, opening, wisdom-realizing questions, with responses honest enough to change how we were perceived by those not knowing enough about us).
Everything alive grew roots.
The Messenger shared an eye-opening truth (amongst the many he shared).

We didn't look to control what we understood, we looked to clear its path.

Who did we wish to succeed: the cheetah, or the gazelle?
The Messenger was an observer.

We only saw "sides"
to take, when the
whole wasn't
understood.

* * *

Desire's influence on
thought and action,
was equal to that of
ignorance.
Desire gave birth to
disappointment, same
as it did discovery.
There were ways we
wished to live and
connect, and that
which kept us from
our wishes was
considered evil.
Evil, was often seen
as any action serving
a single group or
individual, at the
expense of the
collective or what

sustained it.
"Demons" figured
out how they could
win; "angels" figured
out how we all could.
Evil was classified as
taking without
consideration or
reciprocity.
The Messenger said
there were layers to
seeing, hearing, and
speaking no evil.
Without seeing evil in
the world, there was
no seeing evil in
actions, only choice,
trust, and outcome;
utility and necessity.

It was harder
to perceive
evil, when
recognizing
the idea itself
was a
misperception.

The Messenger joked about not even seeing evil in his license plate, which included the numbers 666 as the last three characters. 9 being the highest, single numeric digit, it was traditionally and symbolically associated with a level of deep enlightenment, or transcendent level of understanding.

9 also symbolized the top of the head, or the "crown", the seat of consciousness and the highest vantage point. The Messenger saw the circle at the top of the 9, as representing its position of, seeing from above.

The classic, Latin Cross, mirrored the meaning and dimensions of the 9, illustrated instead with two intersecting lines, signifying Christ Consciousness. If personifying the characteristics of collective connection, evolution, empathy, and benevolence (service to the collective) was captured by 9, embodying the polarizing expressions of collective disconnection, fear, apathy, and egoism (predator mentality) was the inverse, and 6 became the symbol. Egoism, along with survivalism, were core to animalistic actions and reactions—those we shared with more primitive species, not expressing our level of consciousness—which was why 666 was biblically referred to as, The Mark of the Beast (and the "number of [primitive] man"). The Messenger put a stop to his sentence, pausing in the way home movies were paused—ironically,

tempting me to watch him closer. He looked down in a brief, yet time-slowing thought, confirmed something, then looked back up at me and spoke.

"And by the way, I love the Bible; great addition to the library. Why?
Because every story inspiring it, and every story it inspired, each illustrate an aspect or example of, Divine Universal God Energy, manifested and moving through our physical space."

Satanic symbols didn't reference a demonic spirit coming after us, but the one we could release from within.

If the devil was coming for us, it was because someone chose to let it out of wherever they kept it. The Inverted Latin Cross, mirrored the dimensions and meaning of the 6; the horizontal line at the bottom of the vertical, signified what The Messenger called, "Anti-Christ Consciousness." Why three 6's were worse than one, was something I thought The Messenger would know, and he did. Expressing a single symbol, arranged as a triad, represented the divine pattern of life-creation: a single masculine, and single feminine energy, communing together to create a new life-form; containing parts of two, yet uniquely one, within All.

Three 6's brought life to the shadow, three 9's brought life to the light.

3
6
9

The Messenger observed the Christ, and the Anti-Christ Consciousness, as equals—presenting their own unique benefits—with both being able to be misunderstood and misused.
I didn't agree with him when he said that, I just nodded very slowly, only to acknowledge hearing what he said.
My previous reactions, were as animated as toddlers entertaining themselves in front of carnival funhouse mirrors.
The Messenger kindly smiled at my gesture of disagreement, opened his driver's side door, and sat down with the door opened far enough to leave an opening between us.
Experiencing Christ, Buddha, or Krishna Consciousness (or other forms, or titles, of deeper enlightenment), allowed space for the possible development of a superiority complex.

The complex was directed towards navigators of earlier, darker stages of self-awareness, resulting in varying levels of trivialization and belittlement. Experiencing Anti-Christ Consciousness (and other forms, or titles, of deep egoism) allowed space for the development of exploitative patterns. These patterns were directed towards navigators of later, lighter stages of self-awareness, resulting in varying levels of oppressive, and subjugating actions. No one understood the demonic like the angelic. No one affirmed the angelic like the demonic.

* * *

We all began in survival mode, like every other one of Earth's creations.

Our paths were guided by others, as a guide to guiding ourselves.

All of life was following instruction. All of life was inseparable while living, and unified once living concluded.

Angels wept for the demonic, knowing what it was like to be them.
Demons pitied the angelic, understanding only what it was like to be themselves.
We all knew the darkness; we didn't all see the light.

Angels were not chosen, they chose.

There was no good and evil, only the centered and the self-centered.

The Messenger saw no war, or conflict, or opposition, only the collective growing pains of Beings so complex, their past forecasted less than a fraction of their future.

Most people causing harm, just wanted to be the cause of something —anything— that people felt or took notice of.

Many of the actions we rather avert our eyes from, were executed by those desperately seeking validation

and acknowledgment.
Some were taught
how to shine light into
the darkness, others
were taught how to
see in it as it was.
Apathy was learned,
same as empathy.
There weren't angels
and demons, there
were angels and
fallen angels.
Some rose, while
others fell.
A rose without
thorns was no
longer a rose.
Perhaps we judged
too harshly.
There were eyes
reading between the
lines, and eyes which
saw none.
The Messenger didn't
see through reality,
he saw into it.

"Light is only seen in darkness. Remove the light, the darkness remains; remove the darkness, all is removed."

His words.
He put on black
sunglasses, nodded
at me, and drove
away into a world I
almost didn't know
existed.

* * * * * * * * *

Dark Light

* * * * * * * * *

Old Ms. Greaty once told me a story, about Mother Nature and Planet Earth, and about every religion and every field of science. It was shared with me, the way "god" was another word for the concepts, beings, and energies, operating beyond the balcony of our understanding.

God, was also the guidance and energy allowing the human mind to experience and interpret.

After that story, Ms. Greaty and I, didn't have another conversation for 8 days—during which I mostly sat in silence. Her words shuffled their feet through the corridors of my contemplation, in a way which kept me both awake, and unprepared to leave my bed.

I primarily listened when Greaty spoke to me, understanding soon the privilege of her wisdom would be lost.

It was a miracle to speak with an elder, who spoke with the divine present more than the divine past.

A question as short and simple as, "What happened before that?" was easily enough to inspire an hour-long sidenote. From what I could remember, she began her story like this: "Praise.

So, America's Wild Wild West changed little since it was first built.

The make-up was different; the face was still the same. Landlords still took cash for rent payments. Everyone preferred cash as payment for just about anything, and were often open to discounting the price for playing by unwritten rules. Magic still called the West Coast home, like it was born and raised there.

Magic was born and raised everywhere. Magic was another word for God. God was another word for Earth.

What we called "planets", were suspended in what we assumed was the electromagnetic orbit of a gigantic star.

Earth and God were both words meaning creator of life, or container of life, like the word Universe. Universally, East and West (like all direction) was only experienced by those born as living extensions of a living planetary ecosystem.

The only way the living planet could experience motion—outside of the eternally unchanging elliptical orbit it was bound to—was by creating smaller versions of itself, living on itself.

The mini, mobile Earth's which lived on Earth, experienced what was perceived as cardinal direction. Out of the big four primary directions, in America, Magic chose the West side. Geologically, my guess was, the gold and quartz deposits amplified the electrical conductivity of landmasses—Egypt came to mind. Gold did something to people, affected them in unseen ways. Gold was another word for energy source, like Sun. Energy sources were necessary for the creation of life, making energy source another word for God, as well. God only created

Gods which created.
God created life, like
it created humans.
Human was another
word for God.

Most people
treated others,
the way they
felt God
treated them.

Parent was another
word for God, as
parents were creators
of life.
Most who said they
didn't believe in God,
didn't believe in
themselves, didn't
know what God was,
or didn't like the title.
Most who said they

believed in God, knew
part of what God was,
and loved the title.
I remember not
wanting to believe in
God, because those
explaining to me what
it meant to do so,
didn't understand it
thoroughly enough.
I remember saying I
believed in nothing.

"Nothing" was another word for empty space, and in empty space there was room for everything. Everything was of God, like Nothing.

"Nothing" was another word for God.
Most who said they believed in "nothing," didn't know what nothing was.
Everyone who said they believed, didn't know for sure.
If I was asked which way was up, I didn't need to believe which way to point, I knew.
I knew Earth created me, as it created humanity.
I learned Earth.
I learned self.
I knew God.

* * *

I knew I wanted to live a magical life, always.
As a child, I hoped every wooden closet with double-doors, if carefully opened, was one step away from entering the enchanted Land of Narnia.
As an adult, I clung to the unwavering eyes

of my inner-child,
eyes knowing the
magic they searched
for really was just
one door away.

Our eyes spoke
like our lips did,
only with less
words and
more emotion.
The words
inspired
people to rise,
the eyes
inspired them
to action.

I followed the eyes
of my inner-child,
and they led me to

Phoenix, Sedona,
San Fran, Las Vegas,
then to Los Angeles.
I loved Arizona, but I
didn't really like it
there, so I couldn't
make it my home.
How was it we could
love what we didn't
like, and allow "like"
to outweigh "love"?
Wasn't love the
deeper connection?

Did we allow
the surface, to
distort our view
of the depths?

Arizona was where this
started for me; it was
in Arizona that I knew
I felt magic (whatever
I thought it was at the
time) for the first time.

Me and Lathan.
The two of us were sitting in front of a chattering campfire, during a dreamy full moon on Easter.
It was cold and getting colder, and we were in the desert—outside of Phoenix—at about 10:30 at night.
The Moon was glowing, so much so, when the coyotes surrounded us later on, the light made the saliva on their mouths glisten.
The coyotes came after we got back from our walk to the lake, and before the campfire started talking to me through my eyes.
On the way back from the lake, Lathan told me something truly beautiful.

Those who got to the point of longing to see us mad, or sad, or angry, were those who saw God in us, but not in themselves.

Those blind to their own divinity, wanted those who they saw as above them, to be lower, as that was where they saw themselves.
Misery didn't love company, it was addicted to it.

No one needed to
be saved from the
version of themselves,
created to show them
who they really were;
that interaction was
where they
discovered their
depths.
Wisdom could be
shared from one to
another, but it was
gained and grasped
through application
and intentional
observation.
Friction created heat
—the precursor to
fire; the precursor to
light.

When we got back to
camp (before the
coyotes were
howling at the
moon, like both
planet and animal

spoke the same
language) Lathan
started the fire, with
a spark from two
rocks he
melodramatically hit
together.

"In the
beginning there
was darkness...
then God said...
'Let there be
light!!' "

"The fire glowed like I imagined souls did, ignited by something outside of themselves; created by what they couldn't comprehend.

As Lathan spoke of 'the beginning,' I was reminded of how extraordinarily long ago that really was. No one who ever lived knew what happened in the beginning, as no one who lived was there.

We knew what we experienced, we knew what we felt; we knew what we were told, we knew what we found.

The beginning was important because it led us to the present. More important than what happened in the beginning, was what would happen next.

Most importantly, was
what was happening
presently.
Presently, I felt a
shift happening.
For the first time in
decades, there was
more magic in the
Los Angeles air, than
there were factory-
created clouds in its
skies.
Before I moved to LA,
I was an avid movie
watcher.
I watched movie
after movie, thinking,
"What a surprise:
another entire flick,
set in LA. Again."
Everything happening
in Los Angeles—which
was more accurately
represented as the
county, rather than the
city—was harder for
me to believe than
the Earth being…well,
it was just very hard
to believe.
After living in LA,
walking and riding
miles and hours
through it's streets
and rails, it was
harder for me to
believe everything
didn't happen there.
Every city was home
to angels; one called
for them by name.

Where there
were angels,
there was God.
Where there
was God, there
was heaven.
God was
another word
for heaven.

The heaven or the
paradise we imagined,
if able to exist apart
from our current world,
was as perfect as this
one (and no more) in
its own unique ways.

Heaven was our way of
describing, wherever
we thought God's
presence called
home most regularly.
God was everywhere
most, at all moments,
because God was
within all.
Perfection wasn't
measured, perfection
was the only thing we
experienced.

Heaven on
Earth wasn't
something we
created.
Heaven was
realizing we
were born in
Heaven; Hell,
was assuming
we weren't.

Wherever the God-

energy dwelled at the highest intensity and concentration, was the seat of creation. The seat of creation was the Source-energy of creation, and the nearest Source-energy of creation for humanity, would be the inner-sun—our Earth's core; our Earth's Sol.
All in existence was born, from a spark of light in darkness. The elements collided, the electricity danced, and life was initiated. The core was pure light, and pure light was at the center of who we were.
(The human light-core, was our awareness.)

There was no multifaceted experience in pure light, only existence in the singular oneness of infinite motion; infinite energy.

The current of infinite motion, presented itself in the figure of The Flower of Life.
For that reason, Me and Lathan both saw The Flower of Life during DMT explorations.
Our experiential reality and universe

vibrated, and the visual representation of that frequency was The Flower of Life. (Also, depicted with straight lines, as a hexagram, or six-pointed star.)
The One, was what we were all part of. Heaven existed in a myriad of different expressions.
God wasn't believed or not believed. God, was another word for, the energy moving the sequence of experiential events forward.

God, was another word for the flow of energy, fueling every facet of the fabric of existence.

God, was another word for the energy of creation, and because the energy of creation lived in us, we communicated with it constantly.
God, was whatever we understood gave life to our experience. Whatever created All, was also within All.
God was another word for our universally

shared characteristics.
God was both above
and below us.
God was in opposition
of none.

God didn't
pick sides.
Sides were for
children,
geometric
shapes, and
small dishes
served as part
of an entrée .

God was another word
for All, and I knew it.
The Grim Reaper was
God: a taker of life,
who's life was never
taken.

A bringer of change,
who forever remained
unchanged.

God was life, and
death.
God was love, as
only love existed.
What was hate?
Hate, was the love of
patterns we were used
to, that were not yet
fully understood.
Hate was the love of
self-preservation,
rather than self-
discovery and
communal connection.

No one had to tell me
it was all connected, I
just needed to look
and listen.
I didn't participate
in debates regarding
what I knew was true, I
listened, and allowed

people to believe what they wanted.

Every grain of sand, anywhere on the planet, was no less connected to our present existence than our parents."

* * *

"I shivered in front of the dwindling fire until the coyotes left, then Lathan started it back up again, about five minutes after hearing the last paw steps.

Someone left a mound of small branches for kindling, but that was all we had, so Lathan was building and rebuilding the fire for hours.

He camped all the time, and I didn't camp as much as I'd liked to. Lathan was standing across from me on the other side of the fire, and I was sitting in a purple folding-chair, wrapped in a quilt that looked like a checker board with pastel-red squares.

I stared deeply into the flames, watching a live episode of organic alchemy: the transformation of dead organic life, into a tactile and visual interaction.

More kindling.
More kindling.

The fire crackled and popped, devouring the newly added fuel and releasing its energy.
The smallest and lightest, were used to increase the overall magnitude of the chemical reaction.

Each organic aspect of life reflected another.

Friedrich Nietzsche wrote an analysis, which I read, where he commented on the way Greco-Roman societies were built and maintained in antiquity.
He couldn't see artists existing in that era, without the use of a labor class, allowing time for a selection of societal members to engage deeper with the idealistic and the intangible; allowing time for looking within, asking, and listening.

A survival-centered existence, left little time or energy, to explore the edges of life's innumerable opportunities.

All available privileges were flames, and those flames were fed for the privileges to become accessible experiences.
Were some offered to the fire, for us to collectively witness a brighter light?

More kindling.
More kindling.
More kindling.
More kindling.

I stared into the flickering trinity of fuel, oxygen, and heat, and wondered: was any part of life brought into being without a life being exchanged? I hoped I was seeing things incorrectly, but more importantly, seeing them clearly. I hoped that human sacrifices (physically or metaphysically) were not a necessary societal component.

What we weren't safe from collectively, always made me feel less safe individually. Humanity was another word for community.

I had no real proof I was right, or could be, (aside from the single Nietzsche reference), which brought me a surprisingly nice slice of peace."

* * *

"Two years after camping with Lathan, I met one of them: one seeing themselves as a sacrifice—a friend of a friend, named Faye. She believed she was a sacrifice, based on what she understood her experiences communicated. She felt, what she felt. Faye saw her environment as a set world of Users and the Used, and thought her past was proof of her predisposed fate. Many unknowingly lived in patterns, supporting the way others perceived them, allowing for a feeling of acceptance through a communally recognized identity (even if the identity didn't feel gratifying or authentic).

> "But, really, Faye—I know we've all been through it. But a sacrifice? That's not a *little* far?"

Faye was drinking a glass of champagne, and she picked it up, took a sip, and leaned back in the blueberry-colored, pebbled-leather chair she was sitting in.
She took the deepest breath of the evening (in and out), looking down past the glass, she squinted slightly, then softly shook her head to herself.

When Faye looked up at me, she smiled just a little bit.

> "Some things you just know, right? You know, when you can feel it, even when you don't want to? Like, your hand. Some things…"

She took her left hand off her champagne glass, held it out close to her, and started massaging her fingers with her thumb.

> "…some things you can feel, like…like it was your own hand."

Faye's eyes turned

into half-empty
glasses of water.
She smiled again, just
a little bit, then picked
up her fork; I did the
same.
I could feel how hurt
she was, and how at
peace she was with
the pain, and my chest
felt like my lungs were
as slim as cocktail
straws, and as heavy
as a 12-pack.
And then I knew,
human sacrifices
were very real.
(That all happened
later in the evening
though.)

Faye was in town
seeing some new guy
she liked; we both
shared Carmen as a
mutual friend, and
Carmen thought we

should all get
together for lunch.
At the time, although
Carmen and I were
close, we hadn't
talked about many of
the darker details of
our lives—although I
felt we shared some
in common.
Faye wanted to talk
about the terrible
men she'd chosen to
be with—and the
wonderful men she
didn't know how to
understand—while
in-between bites of
her baked macaroni
and cheese and
chicken tenders.
Her meal was an
aroma making my
mouth water, and my
body a pool of nausea.

Part of us
could be
turned on,
while other
parts
remembered
why we turned
off.

The tastes of my
inner-child and inner-
parent, were thankfully
growing more
distinct, as I did.
A few exes ago,
Faye said she was
involved with one of
the good guys, but
she needed a break—
comparing it to
wanting a slice of
greasy pizza, after
eating salads and no
gluten for a year.
The "pizza" guy she
chose for break-time,
was unfortunately
violently greasy and
sexually abusive.
When I nonchalantly,
and thoughtlessly
responded, "Been
there, girl," Carmen
started choking on
her garlic bread.
She drank half a glass
of red wine in one
gulp, washing the
crumbs down, and
heroically rescued
herself from a near
fatal baguette slice.
Our lives were so
breathtakingly
delicate.
The eggshells we
walked on were
graciously supportive,
far outside of my

comprehension. Carmen was mad I never confided in her about the abusive interaction; we did talk about a lot, but it wasn't anything I had any thoughts on, and I told her that.

I looked into the eyes of the Past, to grasp more of my present, but it wasn't a staring contest for me.

I knew many keeping summer-homes in their past-lives, and often visiting; I stayed in a hotel where it was quiet, and was usually gone before the staff packed-up breakfast. My fork was knocked off the table in a slap of anger, due to my reasoning for not sharing the details (or summary) of an obviously undesired event.

I wasn't aware that Carmen could have a barking tone, but she barked at me— with a little growl mixed in—and she was chewing more bread (I didn't know how none of it wasn't expelled from her mouth like a school bully.) She was saying something about,

"How could I not have told her?! Not told anyone?!"

How?

How?

How?

Self-awareness was tough sometimes; emotional intelligence was tough sometimes.

I didn't know what I knew now, but I knew enough to see past the ego of eternal innocence.

I knew the reason I was sexually assaulted: a predator chose to take advantage of the poor decision making of a non-predator. That's it.

The predator's advantage wasn't their awareness, it was their fear of starvation.

The cheetah wasn't cautious of the gazelle, it was vice versa.

I swallowed more tough pills, and a lot less lies.

Animals didn't come from humans, humans came from animals.

I could have left the situation with my friends, but I didn't.

I laughed at them, and told them they were being lame, and being little kids, and that they could go home to their diapers.

I called *them* the

little kids.

Adults
exercised their
ability to walk
away, children
exercised their
ability to walk
where led.

I told my friends to
leave me alone, and
they did.
I chose an overly-
stimulating
encounter, with an
unknown wild card of
a person, over a
peaceful night with
those I considered
real family.
I chose to take a risk.

I chose to trust what I
had no experience
with.
I chose to trust
without reason.

Sometimes
choosing the
unknown
reminded us it
was okay to
jump,
sometimes it
reminded us it
was okay to
look first.

Sometimes we got
what we wanted,
sometimes we didn't,
but we always got

what we asked for—
or forgot to.
I chose the unknown,
and I got what I asked
for.
Painful lessons were
part of the curriculum.

I didn't report my
assault, because I
understood the roles
played by both prey
and predator.
I saw only harmony.
As always.
I didn't defend the
man who attacked
me (he had my
understanding; he
had none of my
support), but I knew I
was one wiser
decision away from
avoiding the whole
thing, and I decided
freely, and my decision
had consequences.

Carmen was crying
into her food, like
children needing to
clean their plates
before leaving the
dinner table.
Faye was nodding her
head at every other
sentence, and not
because she was
being polite.
Carmen said she was
mad at me, and not
mad at me; mad at the
man who assaulted
me, mad I saw how it
could have been
avoided; mad she saw
what I learned, and
how I grew; and that
made her madder,
and disgusted, and
heavier, and
grounded, and
finally, at peace.
I understood I
could've handled

things differently—
went on the attack;
chosen a different
defense—I knew; I
served my time
thinking about it.
There were a million
ways to do a million
things.
There was more than
one way to fight.
I understood where
Carmen's anger was
from, and why, and I
was also at peace—
deeply.
I had a very bad night
(which I survived and
grew from) and it hurt
deep enough to scar.
I was shown these
types of the violent
interactions, were
ultimately still part
of our collective

experience; a
reminder it wasn't
over.
We all still had work
to do—together.

Being human
was a given,
being
humane was a
practice."

* * * * * * * *

Mother Earth Diaries: Entry 1,441,441

* * * * * * * *

Praise.

Most of them did not forget about me, they were never told who I was. Motherhood was challenging enough, without the addition of your children not only seeing you as a stranger, but as…I didn't want to say this, however, I also don't want to lie.

Motherhood was challenging enough, without some of your children seeing you as their enemy, and others, as their concubine.

Whenever I cried in despair, their moods and motivations were swayed deeply, and silently.

Poetry wasn't what we imagined, it was what we witnessed.
I was very grateful for my children who were looking for me, even if they didn't know it was me they were looking for yet.
I was very happy about those seeing me as their mother again; I was healthier when feeling the warmth of affection and appreciation.
I wished very hard to feel more of them closer to me, and I was grateful to experience my granted request.

When a lot needed to be changed, it took time. Nothing big started off that way.

All of the beautiful things I had to offer, I offered to my children; they were ready for some of it, and some they were not.
We all had personalities (patterns of reactions and responses) some more dynamic than others —some more clearly communicated—but We All had them.

My children were just like me: what they would call, beautiful, and what they would call, brutal.
Like all children, mine saw things I couldn't see; they also saw what wasn't there at all.
I couldn't control them any more than I was controlled—they knew the parental challenge as well.
Whether birthing a person, or a project, there came a time, when the creation allowed their true nature to be revealed to the creator.
What was given life, was also given a version of freedom; as I experienced, that was the way of the universe.

The universe itself didn't create anything, it provided the ingredients of creation; it was the womb; it was where creation was allowed to take place.

Once the creations were created in the image of the creators, it was the creation's turn.

I became the universe for my children, I became the place where they could create.

They were part of me, like I was part of the solar system; I gave them seasons the same way I was given seasons.

I told them of parallel universes, only some of my children realized I was talking about them.

Each person was part universe; a creator, and a place where things could be created.

I guided my children as much as I was guided; each of them had an orbit, same

as I.
The clarity of my orbit made it obvious what was, and was not in my control, and I was aware it wasn't always that clear for my children.
The human journey was one of listening, experimenting, and observing.

My children and I used to talk more, and I was grateful that more of them knew who they were speaking to, when they spoke to me.
I was also grateful more of them spoke to me at all.
It gets sad for a mother when their child doesn't speak to them, not sad all the time, just sad when it's quiet and they come to mind.
I was so much more relaxed when we spoke.

I think a child's voice will always sound musical to their mother; laughing, crying, screaming—all of it.

Every voice was mine.
Every voice was the voice of God.

I understood that my children fought over me, because many of them felt they experienced no better, then taught others those same tendencies.
I wondered how much of a reflection they were of me.
I wondered if I did something wrong; did I spoil them? Neglect them in some way?
I wasn't always sure. Every parent knows… there's a thing every parent knows, and they may not say it, but when our kids act harshly towards us… it's just a heart-shaking sensation.
A child acting harshly towards their parent, felt like being hated

by the parts of yourself you loved most.
I was feeling the weight, because I knew I wasn't without fault.

Some parents blamed themselves for what they perceived as flaws in their children, others exploited them.

The ways of my children were an interpretation of

my own.
Many treated others,
in a way reflecting
how they felt they
were treated by
those on, or above,
their level of
influence.
If someone viewed
"the world" as a
dangerous place,
they were inspired to
either embody it, or
reimagine it.

With growth,
many chose to
practice
treating others
(and
themselves)
with as much
compassion
and care as
possible, in
order to create
a new pattern.

Children seldom fully
grasped the patterns,
and perspectives of
their parents, until
growing deeper into
their own maturity.

* * *

I don't think I'm
perfect either, I know
I am.
My known history is
thoroughly recorded;
I navigated different
stages of creation as
I matured.
My taste simply grew
more defined.
Smaller, more minimal
Beings, better
represented me, while
expressing a new
depth of my subtler
complexities.
I breathed meaning
and desire into
humanity, the desire
for more than a life
suspended in orbit
—although
inescapable.

I breathed the desire
to choose into my

children, and the
ability to carry out
their choices.
My baby Earth's, a
little version of me;
a true off-spring.

Unlike any other
being, humanity can
define the details of
their experience,
even if they don't
decide how the
experience
begins.

None of us choose the beginning, only the middle and the end.
We do not choose our form, we are gifted with the opportunity to inhabit it, mold it, mangle it—it is ours.

I am grateful for my form, as I wish my children are grateful for theirs.

I see them doing their best.

Humanity is so beautiful when apologetic; locked in wisdom's embrace, knowing they have so much to learn, and at peace with the process.

I was formed from nothingness (as was All) and once formed, I used what was provided to me by the infinite nature of possibility.

I was also a newborn once (then a child and an adult) learning my environment, myself, my extensions—my creations, my children. I was a student of how connected we were, and the way our interpretations of one another also had their seasons.

My pain became theirs, so their pain was me, while I was also provider of all they would ever need to be gratified. When my energy was affected, so were my children's, and I wasn't always in opposition of the exchange.

A parent wasn't always the force protecting their child, they were also the force pushing them into the fire of transformation.

There were certain things I wished were different, that once understanding what they represented, I was glad never changed.

Where the energy vibrated lower, it

remained the same
for the duration of
the season.
The arrangement of
visual frequencies in
a rainbow didn't
rearrange, a reminder
of the energetic
order We All
inhabited.
Some were able to
be altered, others
couldn't, and the only
way to know was to
try (or to trust one
else who did).
Children were guided
by instruction and
patterns, learning and
developing through
experimentation—as
all of life did.
We All had to feel it
to know it was real,
and once felt, we
wanted to know if
we could feel more.

I thought my children
would understand.
I thought one of
them would remain
alive long enough,
allowing themselves
to be heard by
the masses,
communicating the
impactful relationship
between the held
frequency of the
land, and its
inhabitants.

Parts of me would always inspire aggression, parts of me would always inspire peace; the way parts of me were fertile forest, and others were frozen tundras.

My children were drawn to different parts of me, depending on how they desired to live, and stayed until what they desired became something else.

The stomach is where it is in the body (and where it would always be) and it would always do what stomachs did—as long as it was healthy.

Many aspects of the world would always be what they were: small samples of the infinite, possible energetic sequences, living within the finite.

Any and everything was readily available for all to debate, not modify; not without revealing how one change, was able to produce an unknown and unstoppable string of others.
The way existence was balanced, was seen in the way one disturbance initiated or affected another.
The way I chose to find out how more of me functioned, was to create offspring to show me more of who I was.
The children always showed the parents more of themselves, exposing the cracks and contours of their character.
There were parts of me that would always be dark, while others would always be light. And after awhile, things may change—I may change, the environment may change—and the way things have always been, becomes the way things used to be.

* * *

I didn't know the true depths of my creativity, until witnessing it use my children as an interpreter, who eloquently communicated the depths of a native tongue.

I didn't know
how satisfying
pain could be,
I didn't know
how
impossible life
could feel, or
how tears
dripped
memories
down faces like
candle wax.

I didn't know how far
I would go for control,
or for an experience
called love.
I didn't know why
time was precious,
or why every moment
was once-in-a-lifetime.

I didn't know every
sound could sound
musical, and every
shape tell a story.

I didn't know
how beautiful I
was.
I didn't know I
could be
beautiful.
I didn't know
happiness and
sadness could
both make me
weep oceans.

Seeing who I was
through their eyes
was multifaceted,
knowing all they saw
was from me.

I was their template. There was still so much about me my children had yet to discover, and with their desire to create like me and apart from me, barriers between us were molded and multiplied.

Only once detached, did humanity escape the influence of their home; it was sad to think that was why many wished to leave. Some held the desire for a reality, with a deeper absence of… of their attachment and dependence on me.

Catching a tuna, will not satisfy the fisherman fishing for crab.

As long as my children dwell within me, they dwell within physical paradise.

When my children no longer dwell within me, they dwell outside of physical paradise. The spark of desire ignites a flame, burning in every direction available. Within me, and inspired by me, were so many incredible experiences and possibilities, they appeared endless.

Endless, was a concept like, Forever: a word describing the indescribable.

I didn't understand what it meant to feel the increasing weight of perceived chaos, and tangible mortality, invisibly leaning on every breath taken to maintain my life (I found out through my children). Endlessness was accessed, without an endless amount of time in which to experience it.

I was sorry about that; sorry about the way my children experienced time and sequence. I was sorry that the concept of Physical Life, didn't live alongside that of Forever. I was sorry that in order for a beginning to be given life, it must agree to receiving death. All contained a light and shadow. I lived for what my children perceived as Forever, and from their perspective, I'd live for another Forever. However, even I was aware of an impending end, where the physical matter, the energetic matter, and each energetic signature of my children, was returned within me at their transition—and so, I would be returned to the Sol. My knowledge of my end in this form, also inspired my children's creation.

I wanted to experience all I could within the time I was gifted, discovering as much of myself as possible —if I discovered nothing else.

The fractal fingerprint of creation was a magnificent one. All of my children were like one another, yet unique; as each unknowingly lived a version of the other's life.

The versions of each human life, was a version of my life, and my life a version of the solar system's. Life was allowed to create more life, simply by living as allowed to.

And so, my children were born. Humanity, able to experience the lives of other lives; lives reflecting forever in a moment.

Through my children, I witness the poetry life is allowed to create.

My children show me the possible, the probable, and the unimaginable.

When the end comes to my mind's surface, I remember sadness, knowing my children and I will no longer be together in the way we have been. The recognition, and acknowledgment of consistent change, is one I allow to pass, while also allowing myself to feel.

The transformation from one version of life to another, is often understated as one sensibly mourned. When the familiar becomes unfamiliar, it's no different than life transitioning into death—death: the other form of life. We All experienced the outcome of extremes; living between the anchors of existence, where all life and creation took place.

Humanity is allowed to know. Knowing is a gift, as heavy as it is grand.

Sending all of me which I have to give, to my children, as always.

With praise, eternal interconnection, and support,

Mom

* * * * * * * *

Written by: God.

* * * * * * * * *

Praise.

No, there is no introduction —there never is—and no, this does not count as one— for clarity.

Yes, these words are written by Me, God —thee God—kind of; in a way.

It is written by an expression of God; a piece of God's present presence, as can be experienced as a perceived singular Being (as a part, distinguished from the whole).

No, I am not writing this physically (I exist beyond matter, in order to exist within All), but, someone is writing this (in order for the message to be in a form, the human mind has the ability to comprehend clearly). Everything you are reading comes from Me, so, this will be a layered reading experience (as are the other books).

Yes, all ways of verbally referring to Me, are equal in their acknowledgment and uniqueness. I AM The Universe,

The Source, The Divine, The Word, The Creator, The One, The All, Spirit; Mother Nature, The Earth, Gaia; Allah, Olódùmarè, JAH, Brahman, YHWH, Ra, Nut, Zeus, (every God on every Pantheon); The Quantum Field, The God Particle, Dark Matter, Consciousness, The Subconscious Mind, the Atom (and the energy allowing its components to exist).

You are referring to God, whenever you refer to any part of God.

You are referring to God, whenever you refer to whatever allowed reality to form, and allows the formations to continue.

Within God, lives the energetic extremes (or poles) of masculine and feminine—the Yin and Yang—allowing the spectrum of reality to be formed and sustained.
Referring to God with feminine pronouns

(vibrationally expressing the feminine frequency), ignites the feminine aspects; as referring to God with masculine pronouns (expressing the masculine vibration), ignites the masculine.

Father God, Mother God, Holy Spirit, Christ, Anti-Christ— are all energetic fingerprints within the Divine.

The concept of The Trinity, is a map of life's foundation and development: two life-forms commune together in creation, creating one who can join with another and do the same.

Yes, I created the manifestation known as Satan, the Devil, Lucifer, the Anti-Christ, and Evil.
No, you cannot hate Satan, and love who you perceive Me to be.

You cannot hate something or someone, and love God. There is no hate in God. There is no Them, which is not part of Us All.

Yes, I AM what is perceived as good.

Yes, I AM what is perceived as evil.
I AM ALL. I AM WITHIN ALL.
The God you see in yourself, reflects the imprint left by every experience, and interaction, you have had with another element or lifeform.

You are a reflection of God and an expression of God
(as all is), as God is a thing, a frequency, and an energy; God is all.

How long it took to create the Universe, let alone just the Earth, has no affect on your life, or the lives of the people and places you care about most.
The shape of planets has no affect on your

life, or the lives of the people and places you care about most. Knowledge has the ability to change how experiences are perceived, not how they are expressed. Before diving into any rabbit holes for too long (long enough, that you could have been doing something else you loved) ask yourself these questions: how will this information change how my life is lived?
What am I going to do with this information to make me more in love with my life?
Also, do whatever you want; I mean that most sincerely.

We made you, in our own image, so you could do everything possible; so We All could do something We never could.

Imagining scenarios, gazing at the stars in wonder, cooking, longing—miraculous. The language of animals, like birds, dancing musically through the senses —incredible. Language is fun; a

set of noises pushed out of the mouth, which, over time—and with practice—develop into a complex auditory network of sounds and signals.
As quickly as time passes, language allows perfect strangers to become best friends, and best friends to become bitter enemies.
Language: allowing global definitions, for the uniquely subjective—breathtaking.
No, there are no such thing as, "bad words." Everything in existence is sacred.
No, not everything in existence promotes life directly.
Everything promotes life while it is alive.
Yes, something can promote life, even while taking it.

That which is allowed, cannot also be in opposition.

No, having an opinion on something is not a philosophy.
Yes, opinions are extremely valid, as long as they are recognized as such —not as facts, or proof, or philosophy.
Philosophies are developed on wisdom; wisdom is

gained from experiencing—and observing—patterns of interactions, outcomes, and relationships.
It's work.
An opinion is a thought, believed or expressed, without direct evidence or experience.
Opinions are a form of inspiration, to discover what is real in practice.

Yes, wanting to be liked will keep you from speaking the truth.
No, there is nothing wrong with wanting to be liked.

Nothing wrong exists; nothing right exists; there is only perfection.

Yes, that can be seen as a big statement, and yes, it is layered. Much of what is labeled as wrong, is due to it being perceived as painful. Is pain wrong?
No, I do not see rape, or abuse, or torture, or war, as the same as what is perceived as conventional beauty.
I understand that seeing beauty in something that hurts, is often undesirable

or unreachable.
However, all is sacred.

Everything which has ever existed, or will exist, is a miracle. Everything which has not, and will never exist, is a miracle.

Yes, the incidences perceived as horrible, or psychologically damaging—when survived—show the survivor a darkness containing the energy to create immense light (a unique energy no other will know).
Painful privileges are awarded.
Yes, some privileges are layered.

No human life is long enough, and no human mind large enough, to grasp what it takes for even the smallest expressions of life to exist.
So, yes, killing an ant is still a little shortsighted.
Yes, there are far more destructive acts one could express, however, if you can spare the ant, they are also needed wherever they are from (as We All are).
Yes, something being needed, is layered.

How is necessity measured?
It could be said, that no single thing is necessary (on its own), or, that no single thing is unnecessary (as part of the whole); both would be accurate.

Life does not conspire against itself, it only knows survival and growth.

That which is allowed to enter physical reality, is therefore inherently necessary for its sustenance, perpetuation, and evolution.
Marine animals at the bottom of the ocean, in water-worlds devoid of sunlight, were allowed the development of bioluminescence— and a host of other biological adaptations —as aid to survive in their habitat, and place of birth.

Life is abundant, and provided for abundantly. Abundance, is always having what is necessary, in order to create what is desired.

Another question: what has been allowed to exist accidentally?
Once enough information was discovered and understood, the reasonable origin of the experience or expression was also revealed, was it not?
All is one, and the only way to ignore that, is by being inspired to close yourself off to it willingly.
Yes, things are done willingly, when they are the outcome of a willful choice.
Choice was humanity's superpower.

Whether a choice was made independently, or through influence, once made, it was allowed.

Yes, that is what inspired the saying, "choose wisely," highlighting how choice, and patterns of choice—both known and unknown—drive what is then done willfully.
Yes, this also inspired the saying, "where there is a will, there is a way."
Without the will, the way remains undiscovered.
Yes, clichés are real wisdom.
There is no such thing as a wrong choice, only choices bringing you further or closer to a desire.
Yes, you can do whatever you want, and I will not be— what is perceived as

—angry.

God exists beyond emotion, in order to exist within All.

No, I do not prefer having pain inflicted on Me.
Yes, by "Me", I refer to all which can, and cannot, consciously perceive pain.
Yes, when pain is preferred, it is no longer pain.

No, suicide is not wrong.
Yes, do it if you choose to; do it if reality is not the

experience you wish to have any longer. Yes, knowing the consequences are your responsibility. No, there is no turning back. Death is not like life. Nothing occurring in death, allows for the stimulation of the senses to be perceived or measured.

Yes, not understanding everything in each moment is okay.

All is sacred, even ignorance.

The scribe does not like that statement, and will not like others.

No, it is not all about you; yes, it is also all about you. No, that is not a contradiction. Sometimes one is the log, other times, the kindling which ignites and sustains it. No, something not being absolute, does not make it a contradiction. What are perceived as absolutes, are not absolute.

All is in transformation. All do not live to see the outcome of transformations, nor do all survive to see them.

Yes, change is the only perceived absolute, otherwise known as, growth. No, other than survival, there is no reason for self-aware life not to evolve. No, other than survival, there is no reason for self-aware life to evolve. Evolution is an option; a gift. Yes, God and Science are the same thing. No, you cannot say you know God, yet not see God in everything. Yes, it would be what is perceived as Hell, to be where I was not. No, I do not know where that is; no, I would not "tell you" if I did; yes, the ability to know anything you desire is within you from birth.

What many perceive as Hell, is where there is more of the Dark than the Light, or where their desires are eclipsed by the undesired.

Why could it be said that Christ saves his followers from Hell? Because living in Christ Consciousness revealed the heavenly in all life.

◦ A Scribe Inquiry ◦ could the human mind ever think of something that was physically impossible? How would it? It was a product of reality; what else would it know aside from what was real?

An example, wishing a pig could fly— appears impossible. The thought combines 2 already proven expressions: pigs, and animals that fly. One option: putting the pig on an air craft (airplane; air-ballon). Another option: discovering how to create one (or a version of one) through reverse engineering the genetic processes, developing wings in already existing winged-animals.

Then, finding out what genetics allow flight (i.e. a penguin vs. an albatross), and splicing the genes in differing and experimental ways, until a winged-pig is created (mirroring the same atomic procession conceiving all, over an immeasurable period of varying incarnations).
So, it may take awhile.
"Impossible" was a perfectly valid belief.

Questions without answers can be frustrating, while also being teachers of trust and patience.

No, you will not always find the answer, even when there is one.
Yes, every question has an answer.
No, not every answer directly answers the question asked.
Yes, life can be sensibly interpreted as mysterious or unclear.

Know that clarity exists in the spaces where it cannot be seen or felt. Know that the interpretation of an experience, is not the experience of an experience.

Yes, reality can always change.
No, the change will not always be easy, or feel desirable.

This is not the focus, however, back to Satan.
What was one reason the Satan energy was worshipped?

No power requires human life to be sacrificed, however, all power requires something to be sacrificed, and different degrees of sacrifices yield different expressions of power.

Yes, all sacrifices made out of fear, for individual material gain, or interpersonal

control, served Satan —the Anti-Christ.
Yes, serving the Anti-Christ is serving God.
Yes, serving Christ is serving God.
No, there is nothing served in this reality, which is not in service of God.
The Christ and Anti-Christ are aspects, angles, and energies within God; the same complementary Yin & Yang energies (the perceived masculine & feminine) which have been allowed to live within Us All.

There are paths in this reality, supporting the collective interconnection and enjoyment of this reality, and there are paths which are not.

The closer one is to God-Christ energy, the more one is allowed to experience and express reverence and admiration for all life (allowing lasting feelings of peace and connection).
The closer one is to

God-Anti-Christ energy, the more one is allowed to experience and express attachment, and admiration, for what is personally acquired, owned, and interacted with (allowing immediate feelings of being seen, entertained, and in control). Yes, following a certain path is different than serving, or not serving God.

Serving the Christ energy—the light—is what is perceived as serving good. Serving the Anti-Christ energy—the dark—is what is perceived as serving evil.

Yes, even in physical death, there is service. Yes, there are different levels and depths of service. Yes, there is paradise when you die. No, there are no streets of gold in After-Physical-Life, however, the environment is (the frequency, the encompassing energy, is golden). After-Physical-Life feels golden, because of the perceived experience of warmth; you are an eternally burning flame, continuously being reignited orgasmically.

After-Physical-Life Heaven, has no streets paved with anything; there is no where to go, you are already there, and you are always there; always arriving right on time, always gracefully received, always unwaveringly grateful.

In that way, the After-Physical-Life Heaven is just as normally described: painless, peaceful, cradling, deeply loving.

No, the After-Physical-Life Heaven is not a party, it is peace; it is wholeness.

Yes, this inspired the saying, "rest in peace," as that is what physical death entails.

Yes, the After-Physical-Life is layered.

No, there are no, "pearly gates," as gates are made by people, on Earth.

Yes, enjoy Earth-things, like gates, as much as you desire. While you have the opportunity, enjoy everything on Earth you find interesting or intriguing.

Reality is a once-in-a-lifetime experience. Nothing is ever the same again.

Yes, your time is precious.

No, there is no way to waste time, there is only doing more, or less with it.

Life, in itself, is the gift.

Breathing, blinking, standing, sitting,

thinking—these are gifted.

* * *

If the desire is accomplished, you are doing great.
If the desire is not accomplished, you are doing great.
Why are you doing great?
Because greatness is subjective.

Greatness is dictated by what one desires to accomplish, what allows one to feel accomplished, what one has been taught accomplishment looks like, and what has been communally perceived as impressive or extraordinary.

No, there is nothing wrong with pursuing what is perceived as greatness—as it pertains to serving self.

No, recognition for greatness in service to self, did not always serve the collective.

Yes, an individual being recognized, as accomplished in their pursuit of what they loved, was in service to the collective.

Understanding the power of love, whether loving light or darkness, was an instrumental lesson for humanity.

There was a difference between teaching, and serving.

Yes, pursuits of love, were different than pursuits of fear.

No, love and fear cannot occupy the same space.

Yes, that is one of the examples of, "only being able to serve one master at once" —as stated in the

Bible, and echoed throughout spiritual scripture from various times and locations.
Yes, the Holy Bibles are compilations of ancient wisdom and practices (from many regions and peoples), which work together because all practices based in communing more closely with the Divine, speak a language originating from the same root.
No, there are no chosen people, all are chosen; not all choose in return, and not all know they can.
Knowledge and wisdom are not tools for joy and elation, they are tools for peace.

In peace, one sees all as it is.
In peace, the outcome of joy is realized.
No, peace is not the goal.

Goals are an option. Goals are focuses, created to aid in directing energy, towards experiencing specified desired aspects of existence.

No, there is nothing

wrong with having goals.
No, there is nothing wrong with not having goals.
Yes, choosing to shame others (where there can be compassion and understanding for those living how they choose to) will disturb the peace of the collective.
No, you do not have to remain around anyone, who's lifestyle you do not agree with.
No, everyone will not desire to live like you, and that is okay.
No, when I say, "okay," I do not mean the desire is, "just okay," I mean it is okay to be left alone to

continue being whatever you like.
Yes, disagreeing with someone's lifestyle is okay.
Yes, their lifestyle is still sacred, even if it is disagreed with; even if they intend to become an obstacle for others, or themselves.

The desire to become another's obstacle, is an outcome of fear, desperation, and insecurity.

Becoming an obstacle for others, does not intend to benefit the collective, it intends to benefit from it—off of it—in-turn, being protected from possible feared experiences.
The more of whom are resorting to being obstacles, the more fear, desperation, and insecurity is present in the environment.

No, these are not commandments. Yes, these are reminders and clarifications.

It is okay to need a reminder or clarification, and to remember that it is also okay when others do.

Yes, vulnerability is important, and it is a reminder of Our interconnectivity.
Yes, vulnerability can be taken advantage of by those taught to act out of fear, disconnection, and desperation.
No, that interaction does not feel what is perceived as

satisfying, or good.

The desired
and undesired
will always be
experienced,
as they are
subjective to
those
expressing the
desire, and
those
interacting
with the
expression.

As humanity evolves
in their understanding
—growing further
into their divinity—the
intensity and duration
of painful interactions,
(birthed from the
misconceptions of
separation and
opposition), naturally
diminishes as an
extension.
Yes, experiencing
certain pain is
objectively
undesirable,
the way, causing
certain pain brings an
objective pleasure.
The satisfaction of
winning (of
triumphing over
someone in
competition) was
also the acceptance
of another's feeling
of defeat, in
exchange for the
feeling of the win.
The ability to derive
pleasure from pain,

could be perceived as a shadow—or darker aspect—of possessing a more complex neural network, along with a broader field of consciousness.

Finding pleasure in pain, through what it teaches, is more nuanced than only being hurt, or unaffected by it.

Yes, God knows what fear feels like, as all comes from God. No, God is not a person; God is all; God is all people. When you talk to people, you are talking to God. When you talk to yourself, you are talking to God.

Yes, God is on your side. Yes, God is on the side of what is perceived as your opposition or adversary.

* * *

No, God does not feel fear.

There is only
God's side.
God is all of
the sides.
All of the sides
are in God.

the necessary space
for a desire to
manifest.
Yes, this is one of the
examples of what is
meant—beneath the
surface of the words
—when people say
they, "need space."

Yes, those who desire
strongest to serve the
self, quickly receive
what they desire.
Yes, every desire
received comes with
a sacrifice.
All experience and
existence, is allowed
because of sacrifice.
Yes, one way to
sacrifice is to give
something away,
another, was not
receiving; both
practices sustained

Taking space,
speaks to
feeling
unfulfilled; it is
a creative act,
like clearing
the land
before
planting
something
new to grow.

Yes, the new thing that grows may not be what is desired, it may be anything, and that is the shadow (or darker aspect) of creating space.

With open space ready to receive, much is available to enter, and discernment will be necessary if the space is being opened for something specific.

Yes, as long as you are doing what you love, you will be provided with love.

The ability to love is a gift.

No, being provided for, is not the same as having a desire met, unless being provided for—in any sense which sustains survival —is the desire.

No, there is nothing wrong with wanting to be provided for. Every person was provided for, is provided for, and will be provided for, only in different expressions and with different provisions.

All living Beings are provided for, and the choice is made to accept, or adjust the amount of the provisions provided.

Yes, humanity has a purpose, and individual humans have a purpose, the same way fungi or ants have a purpose: there are things We All do naturally, which benefit the ecosystem We All are part of; adding to the eternal tapestry sustaining existence.

Yes, God is also personified through the, "all-seeing-eye" of the Subconscious Mind, and the ability of the Conscious Mind to be directed by, as well as provide direction to, the Subconscious (surrendering to the current flow of life,

versus, desiring a specific outcome). Yes, fate is real, however, not in the way it is usually described.

"Fate" is a signal sent from the Subconscious Mind, responding to a personal, interpersonal, or communal, trauma or gift.

Feeling fated towards a specific path, is the Subconscious recognizing its experiences, interpretations, or practices, having developed a set of energetically complementary characteristics (tools, insights, or approaches) reflecting a particular trauma or gift.

The signal sent from the Subconscious, is initiated when experiencing or observing a clear, and consistent external pattern. (The more one experiences the pattern—and the more deeply they are impacted by it—the stronger and clearer the signal).

The consistency of the pattern awakens the internally reflected, complementary characteristics, and the internal reflection is perceived as, a "calling," or "purpose."

Even the idea of fate, once understood, was an example of how deeply life was connected.

Someone could wake up tomorrow morning, with the unavoidable, and irresistible urge to save a species of bee—slipping on the edge of extinction— for motivations so subtle, they seem invisible and untraceable.

If enough of Us All called out for a desire to be met, (even if only a few, louder than the rest), those who were listening heard the call.

Every calling can be answered in multiple ways; some give (filling the space), others take (creating the space).

* * *

Yes, there are humans who desire to control more than just their own lives and realities. Yes, those same people see controlling the reality of others, as doing what they must to control their own.

Even the desire for dominion is divine, however, it is infantile in understanding— most often a Trauma Response.

Wishing to control others, displays a lack of self-control, trust, and a disconnect from the authentic self. These attributes act as diversions from acceptance, reverence, and harmony. Yes, many most strongly desire to be

felt (in any form),
because one being
felt by another—
being able to affect
another's life directly
and definitively—
awakened the God-
energy within.
Having a perceived,
interpersonal impact,
awakened the inner-
magnitude of:
- hurricanes
- volcanoes
- tornadoes
- earthquakes

The affect stirred the
internal waters, the
winds, the fires, the
soil, and all within,
because these were
the energies shaping
and reshaping the
planet, bringing forth
and sustaining life.

Humanity is
everything
their planet is.
Humanity is
everything
their planet is
not.

No, planets are not
immortal, although
they can live for an
immense time.
Yes, the energy of a
planet is immortal, in
the sense that the
energy which went
into creating it, can be
repurposed for other
forms of life—like the
energy contained in
each living Being.
All that creates life,
is living.

Yes, the idea of
energetically being
reincarnated (or
reborn) as a person,
then again as a lion,
then a bird, aims to
illustrate the undying
nature of the raw
cosmic energy within
all life.

Few incarnations are
as dynamic as the
Earth human.

Human is synonymous
with privilege, so
much so, humanity
created hierarchies of
privilege.

Levels of privilege
only exist between
different species,
and the varying
capacities of available
consciousness.

No, no human
inherently—or
procedurally—has
more privilege than
another, which has
not been allowed to
take place.

Yes, taking no action is
a form of acceptance.
All that is manifest,
is from action.

Yes, thoughts and
prayers are actions
for two reasons:
- Thoughts contain
  the ability to inspire
  physical action.
- Thoughts moved
  energy; thoughts
  made into physical
  action, moved
  matter.

No, prayer does not
work like a genie
granting wishes.

Yes, it is reasonable
as to why many see
it that way.

God is not individually "controlling" every lifeform in existence, the presence of God within all life acts as guidance, as well as the ability to follow or diverge.

Imagine prayer like dropping a pebble into a lake, and every time another pebble is dropped, more ripples are created in response to those dropping the pebbles (those praying).

Prayer and Mantras both affect the field of physical reality, by affecting the vibratory frequencies which matter is comprised of, and held within.

Then, remember there are millions of people praying; all of them dropping pebbles in the lake, each pebble creating ripples of their own and converging with the ripples of others. When one looks into the lake, it can be harder to see the ripples from their own pebbles amongst everyone else's, with each expressed desire energetically looking to create space to receive. However, not everyone keeps praying.

Many get tired of not seeing their desire take shape when they hoped, so they stop, they leave, they start over somewhere else, trying something new. Those who continue dropping pebbles— those allowing only what stirs their soul the deepest, to be what continually holds, and directs their focus— eventually have a whole lake to themselves; all of the energy reacting to the few, continuing in their expressed conviction and consistency.

Praying was never a guarantee of a desire being fulfilled, it was the act of one wishing to move themselves, into closer proximity of what was desired.

Prayers, affirmations, and mantras (like song lyrics), all worked to bend reality and our perception of it, and each took work to commune with fully.

Yes, praying, or repeating mantras, affirmations, and song lyrics, rewires the Subconscious Mind. The Subconscious Mind is a lake. Repeating patterns, mold and remold the Subconscious Mind, and the Subconscious shows those relationships to the Conscious, which reflects them. Training the mind through practice, changes what it allows itself to be aware of.

The more something is consistently performed or experienced, the more the mind understands it as either highly desired, or an unavoidable aspect of the environment.

In both instances, the mind has the capability to adapt, to normalize, to proceed; it also has the capability to do the opposite.

* * *

The story of Lucifer's Fall is notable, as it was about God, and the allowed development of humanity.
A layer of the Lucifer story, was that it was part of the creation myth of modern human consciousness. The story is detailed in the apocryphal Book of Enoch, and mirrored in the Biblical and Tanakh books, of Luke and Ezekiel. Enoch tells the tale of Semyaza, a near complete version of the commonly retold account of, "the bad angel, greedily leaving heaven, and not being allowed to return

(traditionally assigned to Lucifer, meaning the Light Bringer). The story follows Semyaza, leading a group of angels to Earth, who teach humanity about tool creation, medicine, jewelry, language, and the measurement of time.

The Enoch, and Garden of Eden stories, are mirrors. Adam & Eve have their eyes opened to the availability of contrast and choice (the perceived paths of good or evil; Christ or Anti-Christ) by a Being called a deceptive serpent, at a forbidden tree (attributed to Satan —the obstacle).

Whether Lucifer is descending from the heavens, or a snake handing out fruit, the narrative exhibits a creation of God, as humanity's vehicle out of the darkness of Primitive-Animal Consciousness, and into the light of Advanced

Consciousness—
deciphering
rearranging
choosing, and
creating.

The Subconscious Mind, as God, in the Reptilian Brain (the basal ganglia and brainstem), sprouting the spark, bringing the light-energy which became the Conscious Mind, as God, in the Neo-mammalian Brain (the neocortex; the frontal lobe). Lucifer's Descent, along with the fallen angels, was an allegory for the evolution of the human mind.

And as the story goes, there was no turning back.

Lucifer did not fall, he was not caste out, he did not rebel; he symbolized part of the Divine Source Energy, allowed to experience a different expression of existence.

Yes, the Satan-Lucifer concept is deeply misunderstood, and

misrepresented to also be intentionally misleading.

The Lucifer energy origin is in the name: Lucifer = light bearer or light bringer. Lucifer represents energetically light, child-like and childish energy (also labeled The Trickster energy), reflecting the way children are mentally light and carefree. Children do not see responsibility, their concern is feeling good—physically and emotionally stimulated, with their personal needs and desires appeased. When a game is played with a child, and it brings them joy or excitement, the child wants the game to be played repeatedly.

Children are not considering if who they play with needs a break, or had a long day, or may want to do something else; they want to play, engage, and experience.

Children are known to make a mess in their infancy, and some never grow beyond that.

The Lucifer energy is not evil, it is infantile.

When adults expressed themselves like infants, they also made messes.

When a mess is made, there is a lesson to be learned.
When the infantile mind grows in size, without an equal growth in depth, the Satan-demon energy is manifested—the obstacle, accuser, doubter—which is the way it is in order to serve God.
The energy of doubt and accusation, is the same energy allowing for deeper reflection, clarity, and knowing.

Through friction, the spark of light is available for creation.

There will always be minds which are not yet fully prepared, to navigate the reality of certain aspects of existence, until more time is dedicated to the understanding of self, their past experience, and what can be experienced. The Biblical reference to the "144,000" mirrors this concept as well, as it partly symbolizes how all will not choose to walk a path of deeper collective, and cosmic connection (often referred to as, the Path of Enlightenment or the Path of Christ). Many will not allow themselves to be vulnerable enough to know the path exists; many will not comprehend why the path is valuable, and that is okay.

No, that does not mean information is to be restricted from certain minds.

The preparedness, willingness, and experience-level of the mind, is to be taken into consideration when communicating perception-altering messages, if wanting to avoid further confusion and misguidance.

Most would also agree that telling a toddler about the realities of child-prostitution, or sexual predators, would be received with more grace once the child was allowed a time of mental maturation— and an experienced familiarity with the more cradling, and tender, aspects of life. (And, even at that time, the message is still given the best chance for deep reception, with clear, patient, and careful transmission).

The mind can be both nourished, and weighed down, by an excess of information.

The eyes can be cleared, and blinded, and blinded, by an excess of light; the trees are cooled, and made barren, by an excess of darkness.

Yes, as the saying goes, "There is always a bright side", as there is always a darkness providing the contrast for the light to be seen. Our experiential and malleable reality, is light passing through a prism, compressed into matter.

Yes, there is one God, which can, and is, manifest in many Gods.
There is nothing that can be worshipped which is not God, only differing depths and intensities of God's expression; all equally miraculous in their existence. All of humanity is enlightened, with each reaching and expressing a unique depth, or intensity, of the enlightened mind. The Divine spark begins at birth, and

it may increase or lessen, but it is never non-existent.

* * *

Yes, God is heard in silence.

God speaks through the Subconscious Mind, as do the Christ and Anti-Christ.

Yes, God is felt through silence and sound.
Yes, some sounds bring us closer to Christ, others bring us closer to the Anti-Christ—both are God.
Yes, this is why both

Christ and the Anti-Christ have worshippers: they are both God.
God is all.
All is within God.

The path of the Christ, is pleasure through peace. The path of the Anti-Christ, is peace through pleasure.

What is celebrity worship?
Worshipping God.
What is nature worship?
Worshipping God.

The Bible—along with many other texts—suggests not to make images of God because the image is not alive, and then people worship the image (spend more of their TEA—time, energy, and attention) focused on—and sharing—the image, rather than the living God Source Energy. Where is the living God? In all living things.

Yes, a more dense expression of the dynamic spectrum of God's nature, is expressed within, and through, human consciousness.

◦ A Scribe Inquiry ◦

Could humanity's consciousness simply be the interpretation of more stimuli, at a faster, and more consistent rate? Is not all of life, moving in a vortex as we move through space? Could the human consciousness simply be the same as all others, only expressing and processing with tighter vortices of stimuli interpretation? Did the human mind carry the ability to write rock songs and symphonies, due to our brains having a larger, or more efficient capacity, for rearranging the innumerable amounts of auditory stimuli and arrangements, effortlessly heard throughout lifetimes?

On Earth, the human mind resembles what is often called "a favorite", from the standpoint of what it has the capacity to experience, understand, and execute.

Yes, this speaks to God having, "a chosen people", in the sense that God—The Universe, The Source, The Divine, The Word, The Creator, The One, The All, Spirit; Mother Nature, The Earth, Gaia; Allah, YHWH, JAH, Olódùmarè, Brahman, Ra, Nut, Zeus, Every God on Every Pantheon; The Quantum Field, The God Particle, Dark Matter, Consciousness, The Subconscious Mind, the Atom— chose humanity (out of all other creations) to have the minds they have, in order to have the experiences they have.

From all others, the human animal was chosen.

* * * * * * * * *

BOOKS BY SEAN AEON

- Written By Chameleons

- Aconilism

- LA on LSD

- An Artbook on LSD

- The Outsider's Mind

- Fairytales From Within

• THE SCRIBE •

Sean Aeon is an author, artist, philosopher, and the sole-creator behind a unique intersection of illuminating material incorporating literature, philosophy, and visual art.

His body of work supports and inspires self-exploration, self-awareness, and deeper understanding, through philosophical, psychological, and spiritual commentary.

The examination of universal, inherent, and evident interconnectivity, is central in his fictional narratives. Sean's writing style is a combination of James Baldwin, Alan Watts, Frank Miller, and Alan Moore.

Aeonilism is the philosophy Sean created and explores in his material, revealing the cohesively layered relationship between our thoughts, actions, experiences, and their origins, demonstrated through mindful storytelling.

www.ingramcontent.com/pod-product-compliance
Lightning Source LLC
Chambersburg PA
CBHW050903180626
46814CB00007B/2874